D1607895

All's fair in love and war

By

Michael Jason Adams

authorHOUSE

1663 LIBERTY DRIVE, SUITE 200
BLOOMINGTON, INDIANA 47403
(800) 839-8640
www.authorhouse.com

First published by AuthorHouse 04/29/04

ISBN: 1-4184-1117-5 (e)
ISBN: 1-4184-1116-7 (sc)

Library of Congress Control Number: 2004092839

Printed in the United States of America
Bloomington, Indiana

This book is printed on acid-free paper.

Acknowledgements

God: For giving me the strength and will.

My parents: For always being there for me.

Lori the waitress: For the never ending cup of coffee.

Valerie: For giving me the inspiration and motivation to write this novel.

Donna: For scheduling so many midnight shifts, giving me time to write.

Lynn, Megan: For the time spent editing all my many spelling mistakes.

Chapter 1
May 1998

Well, where to begin. It was my senior year and I was a member of the band. I played the trumpet. I was not that great at it, but I usually was above the middle of the pack. Anyway, every year the band would go on a band trip, and it just so happened that this year our trip would consist of us being on a bus. The more time we spent on a bus meant the more time we would have for initiations. Some people might call it hazing, but we never did anything that was truly that degrading. (Although when I was a freshman, I had to buy a tampon at an amusement park as my initiation.)

There were three of us big bad seniors on the band bus. The first was Matt Hurley. Who seemed to be a quiet kid to most people, but he is the type of person who would always say something funny at the right moment, and if you really knew him, you knew that he was not quiet at all. Sitting next to Matt was Ben Grieve. Ben was, well to tell you the truth, Ben was the type that the cool people would try to ditch, but Ben was always honest and a great friend when you needed one. Last, but not least, there was me, Michael J. I had always thought that I was a loser in high school, but it turns out that I wasn't. I was voted sweetest guy in the yearbook (Which I thought meant that I was ugly, so I had to be nice to pick up girls), and I was friends with everyone. Seriously, I was friends with the jocks, dirtballs, chess club nerds, geeks, and some of the popular crowd.

Now, our band bus was packed with freshmen and sophomores. Hurray, hurray. Of course, we had chaperones, and we had the unfortunate luck of having the band conductor on our bus, but she turned out to be cool with everything. Then, there was the color guard coach, who was also a teacher in the science department, and, oh my gosh, was she beautiful. Most of my spare time during high school was spent with her, but that is another story for another time.

The buses pulled out of the high school parking lot, and we were on our way, bound for the Kentucky Derby parade. We actually marched in it quite frequently even though we were from a tiny town called Oak-Marland, located north of Pittsburgh Pennsylvania. Oak-Marland was a tiny town, but we did almost have two hundred band members. In Pennsylvania, that's a pretty big band.

I had already scouted every female on the bus for my potential band wife. A band wife is really nothing more than someone who has to come to the back of bus for you to kiss once or twice. As a freshman I was "band married" I had to eat string licorice, as did my band wife, and chew until our lips met at the middle of the string. Then we would have to kiss for ten band seconds, which was more like five minutes. Now, I know you're thinking, why was he looking for a band wife when he already had one? Well, she had already graduated, and by band law, that meant that we were divorced. Wasn't I the lucky one!

I knew that Ben and Matt had already picked out their partners to be bound by band law. Matt, being the shy guy that he is, just had his freshman band wife come back and kiss him for a couple of seconds, and I can't remember him talking to her again the rest of the trip. Ben, on the other hand, being the way he was, chose the old "lick the pudding off the stomach" routine. I mean, please, that had been so overused through the years, but hey, to each his own. So Ben had his girl come back and lick the pudding off his stomach. Man that is so gross. I do not think she ever talked to him again.

Finally, at last, it was my turn. I felt a lot more nervous than I had expected to be. I knew that I really liked the girl I was going to pick, but I did not expect this much anxiety.

There were two sophomores sitting together. I thought both were very cute. The first was a pretty blonde, about five foot six, with a nice body for a sophomore. Her name was Lauren, but I called her Smoke as a nickname, because it went well with her last name.

Then there was Hattie. Man did she look good. Hattie was also about five foot six, but she was a brunette. Hattie had a nice body too, even though she was not as developed as Smoke, but there was just something about her that made me want her.

I remember when I first walked on the bus, she smiled at me. It's funny though, in the two years she had been at school, I cant ever remember running into her before that. Then, all of a sudden, I stepped on the band bus, and there she was sitting there smiling at me. Her hair hanging down past her shoulder, and she was wearing those shorts that guys love. You know, ladies, those jean shorts that are just a tad too small, but you wear them anyways just to screw with our minds. And let me tell you, it does.

So, back to it being my turn for a band marriage. The butterflies were still fluttering in my stomach as I called out,

"Would Hattie please come to the back of the bus?"

As she stood up, I could just feel that I had made the right choice choosing her over Smoke. As she walked down the aisle, I could see her legs and those shorts that looked, oh so, good. She was taking stride after stride, getting closer with every step. I slowly moved my eyes up her body and saw that she was smiling and dare I say blushing? I could tell that she was as nervous as I was. Ben hopped over the aisle into another seat so Hattie could sit next to me. I looked at Ben and Matt, and they both just smiled and nodded. I know they were thinking, go

5

for it Michael J, because that's what I was thinking. Of course I was also thinking, ***Man I must be the luckiest man alive to be in this position.***

At last, Hattie arrived to the back after what seemed like forever. She sat down next to me, and we looked at one another and both smiled as we anticipated what was to come. Ben, being the way that he is, decided it was time to start the ceremony, and he began.

"Dearly beloved, we are gathered here today."

You know, the usual standard words heard in a wedding ceremony. And as Ben went on and on, it began to occur to me that I had nothing planned as far as the initiation part (or you might call it the "honeymoon"). What was I going to do? Oh no, my mind was drawing a blank. Then all these options began running through my mind of things to do. But it had to be perfect. After all, I was trying to impress this girl. I really did like her. I knew right off I could not go the route of Matt and just do a kiss. I had to put more thought into it than that. As for the pudding, I just could not bring myself to do something like that because I am just not like that. Plus, it kind of grosses me out, so I don't even want to think about what it would do to her.

"Do you take this man?"

Ben was going on with his spiel, and as expected, Hattie answered with the standard, "I do."

I knew Ben would be asking me next, but I was still trying to think of something I could do for the honeymoon. As Ben was getting to, "Do you take this woman?"

I remembered my first band marriage and the honeymoon that followed. Yes, that's it, yes! String licorice. With excitement on my face, I blurted out, "I do."

To my amazement, it was done right on cue with Ben's speaking. Ben began,

"If any of you have any reason these two should not be married, speak now or forever hold your peace."

As Ben was speaking this line, the smile and excitement left my face as it occurred to me that I did not have any licorice, let alone string licorice. I sat there in silence with a plain face. Hattie was still smiling, Matt was falling asleep, and Ben finished his line. No one spoke, everyone held their peace not that I expected any of them to say anything, but I still wonder, to this day, if someone wanted to say something but did not in fear of us big bad seniors making their initiation twice as embarrassing as usual.

"I now pronounce you band husband and band wife. You may do to the band bride as you please."

Chapter 2

You know how they say a wedding takes forever and the honeymoon ends too quick? Well in my case I have to disagree. Despite all the thinking I was doing during the wedding ceremony, it flew right by and felt like only a few seconds.

After I had just heard Ben say, "Do to the band wife as you please," I stood up and announced to the bus that Hattie would have to…would have to, would have to…My mind was spinning, trying to think of something. ***Wait, I am chewing gum.*** Yes, that is it. Granted it this would be gross and it would drive the health people nuts, but it was all I had so I went with it.

"Hattie will kiss me, and we have to pass my gum between, each other three times."

Michael Jason Adams

Ha Ha what a good idea. I sure hope she thinks so, I thought to myself.

We brought our lips closer together, and she closed her eyes, as did I. Our lips came together, her tongue came in my mouth and took the gum. She opened her mouth to show the ordained band minister. Ben shouted "One." Our lips met again, and I found myself taking charge this time and using my tongue to get the gum. I also noticed that this time the kiss lasted a little longer. I opened my mouth and Reverend Ben shouted, "Two." On our third kiss, I knew I did not want this to end. She opened her mouth and Reverend Ben shouted "Three." Was that it? Was it over? That can't be it. I stood up and said,

"Wait, I need my gum back."

Yes, clever me had devised a plan to get one more chance of feeling her lips pressed against mine. She gave me a look that said, ***Hey, you planned that didn't you?*** Honestly, I just wanted my gum back. Uhh yeah right. After our forth kiss, Reverend Ben declared the ceremony and honeymoon over, and Hattie went back to her seat next to Smoke.

10

Ben and I woke Matt up, and we all discussed how it was for each of us. Matt said,

"Ehh, it was all right."

Ben, of course just had to go into detail about how his stomach was all sticky now. Matt cracked a joke saying, "That's not from the pudding."

It gave us all a nice chuckle. Then Matt asked me how mine was with Hattie. I said, "Honestly guys, it was the best kiss I ever had." (Which was a lie. Up to that point in my life it was second, first place going to a teacher in the science department. But of course that is another story for another time.) "I think I am going to try and hook up with her." I continued. Matt just said good luck and good night. Ben wished me luck and said, "You da man." Ben then clicked off his overhead light and went to sleep.

I could hear Hattie and Smoke discussing something, but I could not make out the words being said. Every once in a while I would hear some giggling from them. After about half an hour had passed, I decided to venture up their way. I sat right in front of them and turned around to face them, so I was kind of looking down on them. (Every guy

11

reading this right now is probably thinking, he's *looking for cleavage.* But hey, they had jackets on. Sorry guys). The three of us started to chat, you know, normal chit-chat. Stuff like what classes you got, where you live, you know, the usual blah, blah, blah. I realized I did not know anything about Hattie, so I tried to pay extra attention so I could pick up something useful for future reference.

After chatting with Smoke and Hattie for an hour or so, I headed back to my own seat at the back of the bus. It did occur to me that I did not really learn anything useful about her that I might be able to use to be romantic some day. Things like her favorite song, favorite color, or what she likes to do for fun. I figured, oh well, I'll catch up on all that the next time we get to chat.

I glanced at Ben and Matt and saw they were both out cold, so I decided to turn my light off and go to sleep, too. As the light went out I found myself thinking about Hattie. I was never really popular with the ladies. As a senior I had only kissed four other girls and only had one girlfriend in my life up to that point. Well, two, if you count holding hands on the bus in sixth grade, but I never had anything that was serious, and here I was thinking about how Hattie could be the one. The one who would be my girlfriend long enough so that she would fall in love with me and not just the other way around like, in all my past romantic adventures. After three years of middle school and four years of high school, had I finally meant that one who was for me? I thought to myself, ***Here I go again, taking things way too fast. That's probably why I always blow it, and why all the girls I've kissed leave me for other guys.*** So I decided to myself, right then and there, I was going to take it extremely slow and not jump into a relationship. Instead, we could date first and become good friends before getting serious about each other.

As the band trip went on, we would talk every time we were on the band bus. We did not hang out together during our free time though. We both spent that with our friends.

Until the last night when we had a dinner cruise, that is. Everyone sat with their friends, and when we were finished eating, people were just standing around chatting, looking like they were not having a very good time. So me, being the trendsetter that I am, decided to go into the middle of the dance floor.

Now, let me tell you, I can't dance at all, but I do know how to have a good time. The band was playing some country song, so I pretended to do a ho-down dance. I am pretty positive that I looked like a complete idiot, but I did not care; I was having fun. I went and grabbed Hattie, who was watching at the end of the floor. I pulled her to the center and we ho-downed together. Soon the entire boat was really rocking as the dance floor overflowed with people. Hattie and I slow-danced together, and as I looked deep into her eyes, I could see how young and innocent she was. I know she was expecting me to kiss her, but instead, holding her there in my arms, looking deep into her eyes. I asked her if she wanted to go up top on the boat.

Hattie and I went up and looked over the side of the boat. It was a little chilly out as the wind blew through our hair. I put my arm around her and we just stood there for awhile staring out into the water. This was my chance to make her fall in love with me, but I stuck to my guns and decided not to kiss her, but to just let the night end. We said our goodnight, to one another, got on the band bus, and headed home.

Chapter 3
June 1998

About a week had passed since the band trip, and every time Hattie and I would see one another at school, we would smile. Smoke and I would talk about Hattie and me during study hall. Then finally, one day after school, I caught up with Hattie and I said, "Hey, look, you want to get together tonight?"

She smiled and agreed to get together. We decided that night to go see a movie, and to be honest with all of you, I can't remember what movie it was. You know, you should never go see a movie on a first date. You can't really talk during the movie, and there should be a lot of talking on a first date. Anyway, at one point during the movie. I asked her

15

if I could hold her hand, and she was all for it. As the movie ended, it was nearing her curfew, so we decided to head back to her house.

As we pulled up to her house, my Will Smith tape was playing "Getting Jiggy Wit It." I put the car in park and I asked her if she wanted me to walk her to the door. She said no thanks, so I said goodnight and she leaned over to kiss me. An hour later, Will Smith was on his third time around, my headlights were off, the car was shut down, and we were still kissing. Finally she said her goodnight and went inside. I headed home.

Now, for the next three weeks, we were not able to see each other. I had graduation and summer camp. Hattie had her wisdom teeth pulled, and then she was sick for a while. All of this did not keep us from chatting every now and then on the phone however.

In my entire, life I have never done anything to hurt a girl. I have had girls break up with me because I was too nice, but I still do all I can to make them feel good and happy about the relationship. So this is where the story truly begins. It had been over three weeks since I had last seen Hattie and two weeks since I had last talked with her on the phone.

I went to my buddy's graduation party. His name was Chris, but we all called him Turton. Turton was vice president of the chess club and an all-around nice guy.

The party was pretty kicking because Turton had a pool. So a lot of people wanted to come to his party. A couple of guys were horsing around in the pool, having chicken fights and dunking battles. This big guy we all call Spankfurt was winning everything. He was bigger and stronger than everyone, and he knew it. When he least expected it, I jumped into the pool with all my clothes on and dunked him from behind before he even knew it was coming. Everyone cheered as I put him under the water, but once he got up, I went under. And let me tell you, it was more than the one time I had put him under. After my severe dunking, and near drowning things settled down in the pool and we were all just hanging in the water chatting. And that's when I meant Lindsey.

Lindsey was about five foot eight, dark-skinned with dark hair, and she looked fairly athletic. We were talking for a while, and when the chicken fights started back up, guess who was on my back? Yep, that's right. Lindsey. Once the fights ended, she sat on my lap in the pool. While I sat on the steps that

17

lead into the water. We talked for some time, I told her that I was dating this Hattie girl. After a long chat, I kissed her on her cheek and said I had to go. She wanted to kiss me more, but I said I couldn't. So I headed out to my car and put the key in the door to unlock it. I turn around and there she was, right next to me, looking at me. "I can't," I said, "I am dating Hattie." But she kissed me and I couldn't help myself; I kissed her back. It was nice and felt really good, I mean really good. It turned out she needed a ride home, so me, being the gentleman that I am, offered to take her.

At the time, I was driving a 1989 Blue Caprice that everyone referred to as the Blue Bomber. Basically, it was blue and it looked like a bomb had hit it. (Believe it or not, the Blue Bomber is still alive and owned by my younger brother). It wasn't like I had a vehicle that impressed her, so I knew she had to like me for me. On the way back to her house, we decided to make a stop at my house and make out on my couch in our basement. Ok, so I know it was wrong of me but I felt that I was only dating Hattie. It wasn't like we were boyfriend and girlfriend. I did feel guilty though, so I must have been trying to justify it.

Of course, the next day, I got a phone call from Hattie, who I hadn't talked to in some time now. She started chewing me out for cheating on her with Lindsey.

"Hey, we aren't hooked up yet," I told her. "We are Just dating."

Obviously she did not see it that way, and she pointed out to me how rude I was. She did not use those exact words, but I don't like to swear, so let's just go with "rude." Now I felt horrible about it, but I also could not deny the fact that I had fallen for Lindsey. I figured I would let things calm down and call Hattie in a couple of days.

While waiting those couple of days, I went to Kennywood, an amusement park. I wanted to win something nice for Hattie while I was there. Well, I ended up winning her a giant-sized Daffy Duck stuffed animal. He was so adorable. After a couple of days passed, I called her and said I wanted to drop something off for her. Now I am not sure if she liked the Daffy Duck stuffed animal or not, but we pretty much broke up right there, and she pretty much told me she never wanted to talk to me again. (I am assuming she did not like the Daffy Duck because I heard from a source that she cut it up into little pieces and flushed them all down the toilet.)

Ok, that night I'll give you three guesses to where I went that night. Yep, that's right, I went to Lindsey's house. We shot hoops for awhile and chatted. Well, let me restate that: She shot hoops and I tried to shoot hoops. (Basketball is not my thing I am a hockey player.) After we were done shooting, I asked her to walk me to my car. When we got to the Blue Bomber, I told her I was single, and we kissed goodnight. On the way home I once again got those feelings of, *Hey, this could be the one.* The steady relationship I had been waiting for. *Stay calm, Michael J. Take it one day at a time.*

Chapter 4
July, August, September 1998

Now, guys automatically know they are not supposed to lie to their girlfriends. Sure, we know this, but that does not always stop us from lying to them now does it guys? So, on my second day after officially being "boyfriend and girlfriend" with Lindsey, she asked me, "Did you ever check me out before Turton's party, or did you never pay attention to me until I kissed you?"

Ok, so ladies, I ask you: Is it ok to lie at this point to make you feel good? No, it's not? You have to be kidding me. Any guy in my situation would have answered the same way as I did.

"Well, yeah, I noticed you in band a couple of times marching with your flute."

He shoots he scores. What a play by me to save the day!

"I play clarinet," Lindsey replied.

Opps, my bad, I thought to myself. So, I continued on to say what any guy would say at that point.

"Oh, yeah, I meant clarinet. They are all in the woodwind section. I always mix them two up."

Obviously a complete lie. Anyone who knows anything about instruments would not mix up a flute with a clarinet. Essentially, that is like mixing up a banana with an apple, it just doesn't happen. Me, being as smooth as I am, was able to make it fly, and Lindsey bought it, I think.

Throughout the month of July, I would drive over to Lindsey's house every day that I could, and we would hang out, make out, and just enjoy one another's company. Every time I kissed her I could feel it in my stomach: those darn butterflies. For some reason, kissing her standing up was better than sitting or lying down. I don't know why, and I can't explain it, but it was the most amazing feeling I ever had. Only one thing I can remember even came close to that feeling, and that was a certain science teacher and I. Lindsey and I even went to Kennywood together in August. When I went to pick her up from band camp to go to Kennywood, I saw Hattie on the way out of the parking lot. I waved; she waved back but with just one finger. That was not very appropriate. At least I did not think so.

As August was nearing its end, Lindsey and I had become very close. My mother threw my birthday party in mid-August because I would be away at college during my actual birthday in September. Lindsey, of course, came over, which made my birthday feel more special. We did not go any further than we usually do, even though it was my birthday, but I was totally cool with that and just tried to enjoy what I thought would be our last make-out session for a while. Even though we had only been together for about three months at that point, I felt like we had loved a lifetime's worth.

When August came to an end, I was leaving for college. Lindsey and I met at what was king of our make-out spot, and we said our good byes. I told her

23

we would talk all the time on the phone and that I would come home on the weekends. So we could be together. Things like that never happen as you plan them, but I truly thought everything would work out. We were just too close to let a little distance come between us.

College began, and for the first two weeks, I called Lindsey every single night. I went through calling cards like they were candy. On the third weekend I came home and we hung out. Lindsey, however, acted a little strange. She just wouldn't get close to me.

"Lindsey, is there something wrong between us?" I asked her.

She replied "Everything is just fine. There's nothing wrong."

But I knew there was something wrong. You could just sense it in her entire mood.

When I went back up to school, I noticed that we were not chatting every night anymore. In fact, it wasn't even once a week. As home coming approached, I heard through the grapevine that she was going with some guy. I called her and asked what was going on.

"I don't want to go out anymore," She said.

Just like that, it was over. As quickly as it had begun, it ended. You know, I am not one to have sex in a relationship, but I heard that her new man got further one week than I did in three months. To be honest, Lindsey and I did not do anything other than make out, but I still loved her very much, and I was fine with what we did and what we did not do.

At this point in my life, I had learned many things about love. Most of all I had learned how much it hurt. I prayed that night for God to help me make it through this and to bless me with another shot at love with someone. I kept wondering to myself, ***When will my time come to keep my heart from going numb?*** A broken heart is hard to mend, but I am learning that, its a reoccurring trend.

Chapter 5
8 Months Later

Eight months had passed; my freshman year of college had ended. I hadn't talked to Lindsey or Hattie at all since my fall-outs with them. I hadn't had any new relationships blossom at college, probably because it took me a while to get over Lindsey. But now, it was summer, and my plan was to go back to Burger King where I had worked all during high school. Sure people knock working at fast food joints, but I always had a fun time working there which is probably why I went back working there so many times. Heck, I was even robbed there once, and I still went back to work.

As work started back up and I was getting back into the swing of Whopper-making, I met a girl named Madeline. Everyone called her May, so of course I did too. May was about five foot four with reddish-brown hair. She was extremely skinny but very attractive nonetheless. Ok, hold up, people. I know what you are all thinking: ***Here he goes again.*** But this time it's not like that! So, bear with me and watch as it all comes together. Everything always comes full circle, and what goes around comes around.

May was always nice to everyone but never really treated me the same as she did others. She wasn't rude to me, but she was not exactly friendly. So me, being my smooth self, just acted my usual charming, kind hearted way. After a while, we began to build a friendship, and soon after, we became really close friends. It was then that May informed me that she was one of Hattie's best friends. She apologized for the way Hattie had treated me and told me about all the kind words Hattie had to say about me (catch the sarcasm I hope). As if all this wasn't bad enough, it just so happened she was also a friend with Lindsey.

Now May and I became very tight, but there were no sexual feelings either way between us, and that's probably why we were able to be such good friends.

One day, while working at Burger King, there was this real big dummy named Sam. I can't even remember what his last name is. Sam was one of those employees who ticked me off because he would just not show up for shifts, like on weekends, and they would let him get away with it. Anyway, Sam had the biggest crush on May, and he would always ask May out, and she would always say no. May always was a smart girl. So Sam came to me and asked me to just hook him up with one date with May.

"Sam there is no way she will go out with just you," I said. "Maybe I can convince her to go on a double-date."

Sam said that he was definitely up for that, so I informed May of the situation with Sam the dummy. I told her that maybe if she went out with him once she might leave her alone. May asked,

"Well, whom will you take?"

I then proceeded to tell May how sorry I was about how things went with Hattie and how I would do anything to make it up to her and have one more chance with her. May informed me of how pissed

29

off Hattie still was (I still think she had over blown the whole thing) and how she did not think she could convince Hattie to go out with me one more time. I told May to just try real hard because I still felt really bad. May said she would get back to me about Hattie, but I could tell Sam she would go if Hattie would go with me. Obviously, Sam jumped for joy over this news and thanked me more than one could possibly imagine.

After about a week of waiting, May told me she was able to convince Hattie to give me one more chance. I, of course, proceeded to thank May more than one could imagine. Due to everyone's situation of past history, we all agreed dinner would be the best thing to do, and then we could take it from there.

Now, I knew that I was walking on a thin line. I called Hattie, and we caught up a little bit. I told her I would pick her up at her work, when she got off. Hattie worked at the local drugstore as a cashier.

So, the day finally arrived for our big double-date. May and I discussed on the phone a way to ditch Sam if it wasn't going well.

"The secret password will be 'Star Wars' ok Michael J?"

Now, you ask why would she say "Star Wars" as the password. Star Wars is a guy thing. Well, at Burger King, I had nicknames for most of the employees based on characters in Star Wars. May was known as Princess Maya, and we had several others like Darth Ian (whom you will meet later), Qui Gon Jim, and Sam Solo. We called Sam that because we all knew that is how he would spend life; solo. Then, of course, I was known as the Emperor. All Burger King employees bowed to my greatness and burger-making abilities, or something like that. Anyway May and I had "operation ditch Sam" in place.

After getting off the phone with May, I began to pray. I asked God to help everything go smoothly, and I thanked him for the second chance that I was being given. Once I finished my prayer, I began to prepare for my date.

Now, guys are a lot different than women when it comes to preparing for a date. When it comes to preparing for a date however, I am more like a female than a male. I started with a shower, and after getting soaped up, I just stood there under the blast of refreshing water flowing down on me. I began to think about the date I was about to go on tonight but also, about the history of Hattie and me. Once again, I felt bad for screwing her over like I had done. It truly hurt my heart to think how I might have hurt her. But that was all irrelevant; now I had the chance to redeem myself. I could make right what once went wrong. Making her see how nice of a guy I really could be was my mission.

I hopped out of the shower and threw on some boxers and socks. I am a boxer type of guy. I need room in that area of my life, and whitey tighties just won't give it (guys, you know what I am talking about). I then tossed on a pair of blue jean shorts and a black belt. Hey, it was summer, and very hot long pants just are not an option when it's that hot.

I then had to choose a shirt. The shirt makes the outfit for a guy. I decided that since this was not a fancy dinner date and we were just eating at the local sit-down restaurant, to not wear a dressy shirt. So I went with my New York Yankees Derek Jeter jersey. Now, you ladies might not see the class in that, but wearing a jersey is like dress-up for us men.

Then came the hair and hat issue. Ok, once again ladies, guys consider wearing a baseball cap as being dressy. Especially if that cap matches the jersey; that is just bomb. So, my option was styling my hair, or wearing my New York Yankees baseball cap. It's a very hard decision, but I decided in the end to go with styling my hair. I squirted a big old glob of gel into my hands and pushed my hair back. It looked like the old greased- back look from the 1950s, but I knew that in fifteen to twenty minutes, it would be hanging down over the sides of my head and looking just perfect as usual.

Lastly came the cologne. I have about seven different kinds of cologne, and I have had those seven for about five years. I just never find a reason to wear cologne, and to be honest, I don't think any of them smell all that good anyways. So, I decided to not put any on and to just go with my natural smell. Hey, my natural smell is not that bad. Seriously. Now that I was done playing around with my look, I figured I would take one last look in the mirror. There I stood, five foot eleven, one hundred ninety pounds, and brown hair hanging down the side of my head. I had the sporty look going, and that's cool, because I am a sporty type of guy.

So, I jumped into the Blue Bomber and was on my way. Let me rephrase that: I got in the Blue Bomber gently, because jumping in it would make it fall apart. (If it had fallen apart, then I would have an excuse for buying another car!) On the way to the drugstore to pick up Hattie, I decided to live up to my "sweetest guy" award, by stopping to buy some flowers. It was a tough choice between roses and carnations, but I decided to go with the bouquet of red roses, with babies breath mixed in.

I pulled up to the drugstore, got out of my car, and sat on the trunk with the bouquet on my lap waiting anxiously for her arrival. Hmmm... It was 6:59... *One minute until she gets off.* All of a sudden, the butterflies arrived once again as she exited the drugstore and began walking towards me. This was it, the moment of truth. Here we go!

Chapter 6
Early August 1999

In all of my twenty-four years of existence, there has never been a time that, when I liked a girl, I have not been nervous about the situation. I have always wondered what causes this to happen, but I have never come up with any answer. I have heard from a physical standpoint that pressure builds up in you lower abdominal region. That pressure, when not released, is what causes the butterfly effect. After a while of the pressure not being released, it turns into gas, which is then, of course, released with no one else's knowledge but your own hopefully.

As Hattie began walking towards me, I could tell she still had not noticed the bouquet. Hattie got closer and closer, then a smile popped on her face, and I knew she had seen the bouquet. I hopped down off the trunk of the Blue Bomber and said,

"These are for you and I…"

Just then, some lady getting into her car next to us cut me off in mid-sentence.

"Oh my, that is so sweet of him. What a nice guy!"

Thanks lady, way to ruin my moment, I thought. I smiled at her, and she got in her car and drove away. My romantic moment had been ruined. Even though the moment was spoiled, I still told Hattie what I had planned on telling her.

"I want you to know how truly sorry I am for all the stuff that happened last year, and I pray that you can forgive me and give us a fresh start. You will always have a special place in my heart, and I hope you can find room for me in yours."

Hattie smiled and said thank you. She never really was one for inspirational words, but I could tell that she appreciated the gesture at least.

The restaurant was right down the street, so it did not take us long to get there. Once there, we saw May hanging out outside the restaurant (probably praying Sam would not show up). The three of us waited for Sam to show up, and we started talking about the Homecoming dance that was coming up in late September. May was telling us how she has a date already, as did two of her friends, and that when Hattie would get a date, they could all go together. Hattie replied by with the usual line from someone without a date.

"I am probably not going to go."

Just then, Sam showed up with a big grin on his face. I can't knock the guy for trying, but man, loosen up a little.

All throughout dinner, it was just May, Hattie, and me talking. Sam just sat there in a trance, not saying anything at all. I kept thinking, ***Man what is wrong with this kid? Seriously, you need to get out more often.*** The girl of his dreams was right in front of him, and he did not even say one freaking word the entire time we were there.

Well, we had just finished eating when May asked me, "Are you going to go see the new Star Wars movie again?"

Ding, ding, ding! We have a winner! Do not pass go and do not collect two hundred dollars. The secret password had been launched and unfortunately for Sam, there were no abort codes. I replied with a simple, "Yes, yes I am."

With that, Hattie and I said we had to get going and May said the same. Sam offered a lame "I'll see you two at work tomorrow." And Just like that, I never hung out with Sam again. It was a good thing, because I found out a couple weeks later that he was all into drugs, as well as other things that are not real healthy for someone under the age of twenty-one.

As for Hattie and I, we headed back to the drugstore so she could pick up her car. As I mentioned before, the drugstore was right down the street from the restaurant, so there was only time for about one song on the radio. Wouldn't you know it, on comes Will Smith with "Getting Jiggy Wit It." We pulled into the lot next to her car. I asked the question I had been dreading all night. Well, it wasn't the question so much, but what the answer might be that I dreaded.

"Hattie, you want to go see a movie or something Friday night?"

She looked at me, straight into my eyes, and said, "Sure."

With that one word, I knew that I was back in. That I actually had another chance to do things right. I wasn't going to blow it this time. I would make sure she was treated better than any woman had ever been treated in the history of men loving women.

There was no kiss goodnight, but that was ok. I wanted to go slow and do it right. With our good-byes said, I told her I would call her tomorrow. And with that, she got in her car and went home. I stayed in the parking lot for a moment and thanked God for this one more chance He had given to me. I prayed that I would not screw it up, Amen. Then I turned my car back on and headed for home.

Chapter 7

As I have said before, you should never go to the movies on a first date, but after talking on the phone for a couple of days with Hattie, we agreed to go see a movie. Seriously though, when you are a teenager, what else is there to do? You can't afford tickets to sporting events, or going to the movies every weekend (what I made in an hour of work at Burger King, I would have to work for four hours just to buy the tickets). My parents are always throwing out suggestions like "Go Putt-Putt or bowling." I am like "Mom, bowling was a thing to do when dad's clothes were in style and Putt- Putt, please, that's so weak, last week." Needless to say, things to do are very limited. This is probably why so many of us make out all the time. It just gives us a way to cope with our boredom and keep us from becoming depressed. Plus, it's a lot of fun to do. Am I wrong? I didn't think so.

Now, this really wasn't a first date for the two of us, so I was not too concerned when we decided to go see a movie. The first time we dated, I could not remember the movie we saw, but this time, I can remember. We went to see American Pie. (If you're going to the movies on a date, make it a comedy. If it's a guy movie or a chick flick, one of you won't enjoy it as much as the other.) We both laughed so hard at the movie that neither one of us had time to realize we weren't not talking.

After the movie, we decided to stop at Burger King to see if May was working. She was not, so we just got burgers and chilled for a while. On our way out, I told Hattie how much fun I was having and how grateful I was that she willing to give us another try. Just then, in the Burger King parking lot, she put her arms around me and gently pressed her lips against mine. It was nice. I liked it very much. When she finished, we just gazed into one each other's eyes for a moment. I was falling in love. We began to kiss again, and again. I said "Hey, let's get out of here."

She agreed whole-heartedly. We decided to find an empty parking lot and make out. She had definitely improved in the last year when it came to kissing and other "extracurricular" activities that were going on. I am not sure if that is a good thing though, because you only get better at things by practice and repetition. See where I am going with this? Nonetheless, she was a better kisser, and I seriously enjoyed every second of our make-out session.

The next two weeks involved a lot of hanging out and of course making out. Every chance I would get, I would try and make her feel special. You know, just by doing the little things, like opening doors, pushing in her chair. And bigger things, like buying stuff for her and writing her nice cards about how much I cared for her. I really felt like we were falling in love with each other.

****

September 2nd

What is love? It's really something that is hard to explain, but I have been told you can get the same feeling from chocolate. Whether you believe this or not is totally up to you. But I know that I have never had any thrill out of eating a Hershey bar. But when

Michael Jason Adams

I am in love, there are so many feelings running through my head that I can't even think of where to begin. All I know is that I was in love with Hattie so very, very much. So much, in fact, that I felt like I was finally ready to tell her that I was. I decided to plan a special evening for her and see how it went, before I would tell her.

I began this special evening by picking her up at her house. I told her how beautiful she looked and handed her a single red rose. Let me tell you something, guys: Sometimes, one rose can say as much as a dozen. Hattie's mother told me how sweet I was and shipped us off, telling us to have a good time. We hopped into the Blue Bomber (after I opened and closed the car door for her) and headed to the Runway.

The Runway was a classy restaurant where you definitely would not walk in to eat in just jeans. I have always wondered, what makes a restaurant classy? I am sure there are a bunch of little things that you girls notice about it that makes it that way for you. For guys, though, the only thing that makes a restaurant classy is the bill. We would be just fine eating at McDonalds, but we have to impress you. So, a fifty-dollar bill for two people is what I considered classy. You know, they charged me extra money for the cheese they sprinkled on my salad. A dollar seventy-five extra for freaking shredded cheese. Oh, and they don't tell you this on the menu, by the way. If they would have sprinkled salt and pepper on my salad, the bill probably would have been sixty dollars. I mean, jeez, do I get a free toaster with this meal or what? Despite the bill, it was a very nice meal, and I could tell that Hattie appreciated the effort I was putting out for the date. How could I tell you ask? I think it was her hand rubbing my thigh under the table, but I can't be absolutely positive about that.

After dinner, we progressed into part two of my planned romantic evening. We headed to the lake at North Park. When we arrived, I popped the trunk on the Bomber (hard to believe the popper still worked on the Bomber) and removed a loaf of wheat bread. Hattie and I walked out on the dock together, holding hands. We sat on one of the benches and talked as we fed the ducks and swans. Those swans sure are pretty animals (and girls just die over them). Once the bread ran out, the ducks quacked at us a few times. I am sure that in duck language, they were cursing us out for running out of food.

Now that we were done feeding the ducks, we began to go for a walk around the lake. The moon was in the sky as it was getting dark out, and the air was becoming chilly. I noticed Hattie give a little shiver.

"Where are my manners?" I explained.

I wrapped my jacket around her to help keep her warm and then once again took her hand in mine. Once we made it back to the docks, we got back in the Blue Bomber and took off.

Sitting in the car outside her house, I was debating over and over again in my head, *Should I tell her I love her, or should I not?* She kissed me and said goodnight.

"Good night." I replied.

Right back to her. Wait, that's it. That's all I have to say? *What am I waiting for?* I thought to myself. Hattie shut her door and was walking to her front porch. I kicked open my door, "Hattie wait," I said.

She stopped and turned around. Then I said it.

"Hattie, I am in love with you."

Chapter 8

She began walking back towards me. She looked me in the eyes and said, "Michael J, will you be my date for Homecoming."

Not the exact response I was looking for, but I felt that it was a good sign. I eagerly answered, "Absolutely."

We kissed, and then she went inside.

****

One Week Later

Word got out to May that I would be joining her group at Homecoming. As soon as she found out, she called me up.

"Michael J, I got to tell you something. Our group is pretty big with my date, you and Hattie, and Chrissie and Ian." (We all know Ian as "Darth Ian" from Burger King).

"Oh, and Michael J, there is one other couple coming."

I was like, "Ok no problem, who?" I asked.

"Lindsey and her boyfriend."

Ok problem. Big problem. Are you freaking insane? Ok, so I did not say that, but you can damn well better believe that is what I was thinking. Instead I answered with, "Ok."

May asked me if I was sure that was all right.

"Yes, it is no big deal."

I wondered if May could tell that I was lying?
Obviously, I wasn't over Lindsey yet. It's hard to believe that I still cared so deeply for her. Maybe it was the initial shock of hearing her name for the first time in a long time, or maybe I just wanted her back so bad I could taste it. Even with those thoughts, I

did not lose sight of the fact that I now had fallen in love with Hattie.

"Anyways Michael J, Hattie and I just got back form the mall. She bought a dark red dress with a see-through black cover."

"All right, May, that sounds good," I said in monotone. We exchanged our good-byes and hung up.

Lindsey. Just saying her name made me feel all hurt inside. How could I be expected to spend an entire evening with Lindsey after she stepped on my heart? I had made up my mind I would call May back right that instant and give her my true feelings on the situation.

Immediately, I dialed May's number. The phone rang once. What was she waiting for? Pick up already! A second ring. I began tapping my foot repeatedly off the ground. Then a third ring. What the…? Finally, she answered the phone.

"May, it's Michael J."

Just then, I thought to myself how I should act my age and not ruin their senior Homecoming dance. But I had to have a reason for calling, so I blurted out the first thing I could think of.

"How about we have the after-party at my house, and everyone can crash at my place."

May said she was definitely up for that and she would let everyone know. Once again, we said our good-bye to one another and hung up.

All right, I knew I had to get Lindsey off the brain, and the best way to do that was by concentrating on Hattie. Hattie and I would be the best-looking couple there, I decided. I had to make sure that Hattie and I would out-do Lindsey and her date. I had to! What else could I do to show Lindsey that she had made a mistake by leaving me?

My mother has given me a lot of advice over the years that has come in handy. Today would be no different. I told my mother what color dress Hattie would be wearing. Dark red with a black see-through cover. I told my mom how badly I wanted to look better than any couple there. Mom told me she would take care of the corsage, but that I would have to go out and get a nice button-down dark red dress shirt and a black tie. See, moms always think ahead. She knew that I already had a black sports jacket (pretty sweet hey?). My friends, I tell you, always treat your mother well, because she will always be there when you need her.

So, with the attire out of the way, I could focus on other areas. Transportation. Sure the Blue Bomber could hold a few people (assuming they did not fall through the floor), but with a large group like ours, I figured I could borrow my parents mini van.

With Homecoming dances come pictures. Moms and dads surround you with cameras, and you sit there and smile like you are enjoying it. Personally, it makes me feel like I am trapped in a zoo, with all these people just looking at me but that's just my personal opinion. Anyways, I found a nice spot in our front yard where all you would be able to see in the picture were these two pretty maple trees (maybe they were oaks I don't know trees real well) and freshly cut green grass (as soon as I cut it, of course).

Everything was starting to come together. The week before the dance, Hattie and I went shopping for my dress shirt and tie. We picked up some videos and food for the after-party and, of course, made out when we were done. We hung out every day that week, always coming up with some

Homecoming excuse so we could see one another and be together.

As the big day got closer, everyone was fretting over little things like where to eat, what time to meet? So we all agreed to make reservations at the Old Boat House restaurant for six-thirty. They called it the Old Boat House because it was old and the inside looked like a wooden ship. If you remember what I said before about classy restaurants, the same holds true for the Old Boat House. Reminder to self: Do not get sprinkled cheese on my salad. Now, up to that point, I had never actually eaten at the Old Boat House, so I should not have been passing judgment on it just yet. With the dinner reservation, set everything was primed and ready to go.

****

Night before Homecoming

Ring, ring, goes the phone. Oh man, what now?

"Hey, Michael J, it's me."

That would be May, for all you who did not pick up the phone.

"What's up, May?"

"Well, I was just talking with Lindsey and uhh…."

"What now?" I replied.

"She is a little nervous that you might be mad at her or something."

"Why would I be mad?" (Yeah, why would I?)

"Well, she thinks you might be a little jealous if you see her with her new guy."

"Is that a fact, May? Why would I be jealous? I am taking the best-looking girl to Homecoming?"

"Well, she is convinced that you might do or say something, and now she is thinking of going without us. Could you please call her and tell her it will be all right?"

"You want me to call her!"

"Yeah, could you Michael J?"

"You know, May, that I would never do or say anything to ruin the evening."

"Yeah, I know, but she needs to hear it from you."

"May, you do know I haven't talked to her in a very long time."

"No, it's ok. She said you can call her. Please do it, ok?"

"All right. I'll call."

Oh joy, just what I wanted to do.

"I'll see you tomorrow. Michael J, we are going to have so much fun!"

"I am sure we will. I'll talk to you later."

Oh boy, here we go. This party is just getting started. I have to call Lindsey. You got to be playing me, because that is not even cool. I reached for the phone that I had just hung up. I took a breath of air and turned the phone on. Then I began pacing back and forth trying to find some words that I could say to her. I shut the phone off. *Hmmm... I need something comforting, yet to the point that I am over you and it's not a big deal that you are coming. Hey wait that will work.* "I am over you and it is no big deal that you are coming."

I said it out loud. All right, now I am ready to rock and roll. I turned the phone on and dialed the number right up. Who would have thought after all this time I still knew her phone number by heart? By heart-nice choice of words, hey? The phone rang once and I began to pace yet again. Another ring went by and excitement began to fill me as I was thinking she was not at home. Just as I had that thought, I heard,

"Hello."

"Yeah, hi, is Lindsey there?"

"Just a second."

I awaited anxiously. I was going to tell her how it was, screw comforting.

"Hey, this is Lindsey."

55

Chapter 9

I had not heard that voice in quite some time. Just the sound of it brought back so many good memories. To me, hearing her voice made me want her all over again.

Is that wrong of me?

Do you ever really stop loving someone?

I don't think that you do, because the pain is always going to be there. If just the sound of her voice was doing that to me, how was I supposed to deal with seeing her for an entire evening with another guy? Then letting her and her date crash at my place afterwards? I don't think so. All right, I know all of you are waiting for me to say it, so yes: I was still in love with Lindsey. I'll always be in love with her; she was my first love (I never went with Hattie long enough the first time to fall in love with her. I just liked her a lot on the band trip, and thought I could fall in love with her, turns out I was right). You never forget your first broken heart, and it will always be there for me. That does not change the fact that I was in love with Hattie, but it certainly does not make things easy, loving two women.

"Hey, this is Lindsey."

"Hey, it's Michael J."

There was a moment of silence. Maybe she did not think I would have the testicular fortitude to call, or maybe she was thinking the same thing I was thinking about hearing her voice. I'll never know, but I still wonder to this day what caused that moment of silence.

"Oh, how are you, Michael J?"

"Let's get right to the point of me calling."

"All right, go ahead."

"Do you really think that I am that jealous of you, that I would cause a scene or something like that?"

"I don't know, Michael J. I thought you might still be mad about the way I broke up with you."

"Well, Lindsey, I can't exactly say I am ok with it, but I would never do anything to ruin someone's evening. You, of all people, should know that. You have spent enough time with me to know that much."

"So you are not mad then?"

"What did I just say? Were you not paying attention?"

"You certainly sound mad or upset to me."

Oh my gosh, can you believe the audacity of this girl? What was she trying to do to me?

"Look, Lindsey, sure I am mad. You yanked my heart out and stepped on it. I loved you, I still love you, and if you wanted to take me back, I would do it in a second. That is just the way it is and the way it will always be for me when it comes to you.

I have to learn to deal with it, but I promise you I will not do anything to mess things up. If that's not good enough for you, I don't know what to tell you then."

Ha, what you got to say to that? I guess I just told her. I think I told her. I awaited her reply with great anticipation. Maybe she would tell me she loved me back, too. She could tell me how sorry she was for breaking up with me.

"Ok, Michael J, you're right. I should trust you. I'll see you tomorrow."

That was it. That's all she had to say to me for spilling my guts out everywhere. It felt like she had stepped on my heart all over again. I just knew that somehow I was going to come out of tomorrow night looking like the bad guy. I could just feel it inside. Well, I decided to myself that there was nothing I could do about it except be myself and try to ignore Lindsey and her date as much as I could. That would be the best way to go: ignore them as much as possible.

It was getting pretty late so I decided to retire for the evening. I had so many things on my mind. I thought about Lindsey and the two different outcomes that could occur. I figured, if I played it cool, all would go well, but if not, then Lindsey and her date would probably leave. Hattie would get ticked cause she would figure I liked Lindsey still. May would be upset because I promised her I would play it cool. If she got angry, then her date would have to go comfort her. That would just leave me, Ian, and his date Chrissie. Fortunately, Ian and Chrissie both were very cool people. They both also knew the history of what was going on.

Ian looked up to me at work because I could always make him laugh when we were getting slammed with orders. Ian was a handsome-looking guy, tall and skinny, and his girlfriend Chrissie was very good-looking, as well. The two had been dating for almost two years. However, Chrissie's parents were very strict when it came to boys. Even with Ian, after two years, they were still really iffy with him. Because of her parents, they were not going to be allowed to crash at my place for the after-party. Although Ian did inform me that he and Chrissie would at least come over for a little while after the dance. I was down with that, figuring it was better than nothing.

Just as I was about to doze off, one last thought jumped inside my head. That thought was of Hattie.

I was so happy to have that thought of her. I knew that even though I cared very deeply for Lindsey, I was in love with Hattie. The person you love should be the first thought you have in the morning and the final thought you have before you fall asleep. With a smile on my face, I passed out.

Chapter 10
The Day of Homecoming

The big day had finally arrived. As I awoke in the morning, I could feel the excitement. Even though I had been to several Homecomings and two proms already, that did not change how excited I was. But before I could get too excited, I had a long day ahead of me. Fortunately, I was able to get off from Burger King for the day.

Unfortunately, I was not able to get off from my side job, which was coaching T-Ball for four and five-year-olds, followed by Kindergarten Flag Football. Neither of these jobs paid very well, but I would have done them for free (in fact, I had a few times). That's how much I truly enjoyed doing them. The only thing about them: I do not like is that

Michael Jason Adams

they are every Saturday morning, and it's very hard
to get off when you are the coach. Besides work,
there were a lot of things to do that day, and I had to
make sure they all got done. I decided to write out
my day so as not to forget anything. Not that I am a
forgetful person, but I just wanted everything to run
smoothly.

> 10:00AM to 12:00PM - T-Ball.
> 12:00PM to 2:00PM - Kinder Flag Football.
> 2:15PM - Pick up corsage from florist (they
> close at three.)
> 2:30PM - Cut grass for pictures. Rake leaves.
> 3:30PM - Shower, shave, get dressed.
> 4:00PM - Call restaurant to double check
> reservations and directions.
> 4:05PM to 4:35PM - Hair. (Hey, it takes a
> while.)
> 5:00PM to 6:00PM - Pictures.
> 6:00PM to 6:30PM - Drive to Old Boat House.
> 6:30PM - Dinner.
> 7:30PM to 8:00PM - Drive to dance.
> 11:00PM - Dance over. Head to party at my
> house.

As you can see, I had a lot on my plate to worry
about. I looked at the list and checked it twice,
and yes, I found out I had been naughty, not nice.

64

Somehow, I had forgotten the most important thing: my date. I had forgotten that I told her I would pick her up, even though her parents were coming to take pictures at my house. Now I would have to squeeze that in between hair and pictures. Like that was going to happen. Guys, you know what I am saying. When has a girl ever been on time for something as extravagant as Homecoming? This was definitely going to be cutting things close.

The day started as planned with T-Ball. Now, I don't know if any of you out there reading this book have ever dealt with young children or not. It is very hard to keep their attention on you. The key, though, is to keep your attention on them. T-Ball bats can be very dangerous when you are not paying attention to them. Let's remember, I am a guy. These children come up to about my waist. They were swinging the bat around me, because I was in charge of the tee. So, if I do not pay attention to the bat when they swing and miss the ball, well, let's just say they still get a hit. To my fortunate luck, I was on today and saved myself from a lot of hurt. If you know what I mean.

As Kindergarten Flag Football started, my mind was already thinking about the Homecoming dance. I had heard from May that this year's theme was

"Millennium." I guess with the year 2000 only three months away, they thought it fitting. I can guarantee you that we were not the only school to pull that one. Anyways, I thought back to my Homecomings from the past and how nicely decorated everything was. A lot of people put in a lot of time to make it that way for us, and I never really appreciated it until then, when I was out of high school and heading into my sophomore year of college. I couldn't wait to see how they would decorate for the Millennium.

When Kindergarten Flag Football ended, I cleaned up. Hopped into the Blue Bomber and took off. When I arrived at the florist, there was a small line awaiting me. Apparently I wasn't the only one going to Homecoming that night. Everyone in line was picking up corsages for their dates. Once I got to the front of the line, I gave the lady my name. She turned around and pulled out the corsage my mother had ordered. It was a wrist corsage with tiny red roses, black ribbon, and babies breath. Mom always was good with those types of things. Man, she was awesome: I should really tell her that a little more often. After paying the bill, I got back in the Blue Bomber and took off again.

Immediately when arriving at home I got the riding mower out and began mowing. For a day late in September, it was quite nice out. There was a little chill in the air, but the sun was shining and not a cloud was in sight. I took the weather as a good sign of things to come. After the mowing was through, I raked up all the leaves and bagged them. Well, to be honest, I did not rake them all. Only the ones that were around the area where we would be taking pictures. So, I cheated a little bit; sue me. I was pressured for time, and my hair needs time, let me tell you.

At this point, it was 3:45. I was fifteen minutes behind where I needed to be. I called Hattie and told her that I was backed up, so if she could just come over when her parents came over, it would be a great help to me. She was cool with it and mentioned she probably would not be ready by the time I was supposed to come get her anyways. Now there was a big shock.

Since I had the phone in my hands anyways, I decided to call and check on the reservations now, instead of waiting until after my shower like I had originally planned. Thankfully everything checked out with the reservations. I also double-checked on the directions, just to make sure. Better safe than sorry, a good motto to live by.

It was now just about 4:00 and, so far, all was well. I laid my suit out on my bed and headed to the shower. Since it was a special night, I ditched the usual Suave shampoo and used some hair salon shampoo I had put away for special occasions. I got myself lathered all up and followed that by rinsing myself off. After toweling off, I cut my toenails and fingernails, shaved, Q-tipped my ears and belly button, brushed and flossed my teeth, and finally rinsed with mouthwash. That left the most important thing: my hair. As I stared into the mirror for a moment, I realized something: I was telling you all about this while I was still naked. So I threw on some boxers. There we go, that's better.

I took a nice-sized glob of gel and slicked my hair back. I ran my hands through it a couple of times to work in the gel.

Back to the bedroom to get dressed. I threw the black pair of socks on, followed by black slacks. Then my dark red button-down dress shirt. I tucked it in then put my black belt on. I then tossed my freshly polished dress shoes on (thanks to my brother, who was a cobbler at the time). It took me two times to get the tie tied right, but it finally looked perfect.

Back to the bathroom to check the hair. It was lying just right. I did not want it to fall or move anymore, so I grabbed my hairspray and sprayed it enough that you would need a chisel to get though it. Don't worry, ladies, it looked good. Trust me on this.

Back to my room. I grabbed my black sports jacket and threw it on. Dang I looked good, definitely the total package. Just in time, too, because it was now 4:55. Almost picture time. I was getting pretty excited at this point. If Hattie looked half as good as I did, we were going to be the finest-looking couple there.

Now, I told everyone to get to my house by 5:00, thus leaving an hour for picture taking. I also knew that we only needed an half an hour for pictures. As I said before, you girls are never on time for something like Homecoming.

Ian and Chrissie arrived at five-o-clock. Chrissie had a blue evening gown on. Ian had a black sports coat, two, but he had a blue shirt on to match his lady. Ian and I looked like two Italian mafia men, But good nonetheless. They were followed by May and her date, Jeff, as well as Lindsey and her date, Bill, who where in the back seat. This was the moment of truth, to finally see Lindsey again. Could I survive, or were there still tears left to cry?

May was dressed in a spaghetti strap dress that was like a pine green color. She looked very attractive, and I could tell how excited her date was to be with her. As he should have been because May is a wonderful girl. Lindsey stepped out of the vehicle. I braced myself for pain. To my shock, I did not feel the same. Lindsey was wearing a black and white gown, and she did not look all that good in it. I noticed I was not hurting inside, even though I was still feelings things for Lindsey. I felt the love I had for her, but I felt like it was ok, everything was cool. Maybe these feelings were brought on by me being upset with her, or maybe I was truly in love with Hattie. I'll never know, but I do know that I'll never forget the time that I spent with Lindsey.

All of us exchanged our hellos. Their parents arrived in a vehicle right behind them. I took them up to the spot in the yard where pictures would be taken. My parents were already waiting as all the adults began to mingle.

At last, Hattie's parents pulled into the driveway. I walked down to her car. As she opened up her door and made her way out, I could see how stunning she looked. Her hair was kind of pulled back, but she had two curls coming down the side of her face (gosh, do I like that look). As she stood and looked at me, I said to her, "Hattie, you take my breath away. You truly are beautiful."

Her dress was also a spaghetti strap. It was a very dark red, almost the perfect match to my dress shirt. It had the black see-through over the red. Wow, did she look great. I took her hand and led her up to the designated picture-taking area.

We all lined up next to our dates as the pictures began. All our parents were clicking away, using flashes even though it was sunny out. The pictures started with all of us in a group. Then we did individual couples. This was followed up by all the girls, then all the boys. The girls did their one picture showing leg, so obviously we guys could not be shown up. We showed our legs too and might I say we looked good doing it? Finally, we got back with our dates and did a few more individual pictures. I once again told Hattie how pretty she looked and how good of a time we were going to have. As the pictures were finishing, I asked May to join me for one picture of just the two of us. We put on our biggest smiles, then hugged one another and went back to our dates. It was just about 6:00 and time to leave. Oh boy I almost forgot Hattie's corsage. I put it on Her wrist, and she said it was very pretty. She then pinned the boutonnière on to me and kissed me right after. "All right, guys, pack into the van."

Fortunately, my van fit eight people, which just happened to be how many of us there were. Everyone but Hattie and I were in. She was riding shotgun. I opened her door for her. As she got in I just looked at her and thought of how lucky I was to be with her. I closed her door, got in the driver's side, and announced to the gang, "Ok we are off."

Chapter 11

The band Jefferson Airplane said it best. ***Don't you want somebody to love***? Is that not what everyone wants? It seems like such a little thing, just one word: love. It's love, though, that usually decides when I am happy. As I drove the Mini-van with the Homecoming gang inside, thoughts of love flowed through my brain. I glanced over at Hattie, and I couldn't wipe the smile off my face. All the girls were chatting about their dresses and hair-dos. All the guys were talking about how much the Pittsburgh Pirates sucked (I have to agree with that, but I am still a fan). And I was just driving and thinking to myself about how much I was in love. For so many years of my life, that had been all I wanted. It seemed that, at last, I had finally found it.

There were two things that were unclear to me and that had been bugging me. So I decided to ask and find out the answer.

"Hattie, can I ask you something?"

She ended her conversation with the ladies about dresses. They had been talking about that for twenty minutes already.

"How is it that you are friends with Lindsey now?"

"Well, when you guys broke up, Michael J, I eventually started talking to her again and I forgave her."

"So, you forgave her but would not even acknowledge my existence."

"Well, yeah, see, I really like you, and it hurt me when you did what you did."

"I am so sorry for that, you know."

"I know you are, and I have forgiven you, too, now."

74

"Ok, I got one more question if it's cool?"

"Yeah, go ahead."

"Did you really cut the Daffy Duck stuffed animal I gave to you up into little pieces and flush them down the toilet?"

"Yeah, I did," she replied as she chuckled.

"Oh, man," I replied with the same chuckle back.

"Ok, that's all I wanted to know. Thank you for your honesty."

She took my hand and held it the rest of the way to the restaurant.

The Old Boat House restaurant was on the corner of two streets. There were no parking lots anywhere to be found, so we had to drive around until we found an open spot on the street. Of course, I let everyone out before I started looking for a parking spot. Ian decided to come join me. I am glad that he did, because I did not get to park exactly close. On our walk to the restaurant, Ian and I talked about how well everything was going, despite all the history between everyone. I agreed with him and thanked god for everything going so smoothly up to that point.

Everyone was waiting for us as we entered the Old Boat House. As we all sat down, everyone began to look over the menu. I noticed that the water had a name to it. Oh great, the water has a freaking name. ***Gee, how much is this going to cost me***? I thought to myself. Hattie told me that she had no idea what she was going to get. I told her that I recommended the senior citizen steak, because they chew the meat off the bone for you. Everyone began to laugh, and it kind of lightened the mood a little bit.

Have you ever noticed that when you are a younger person that waiters do not pay as much attention to you as they do to all of their adult customers? I know they feel they will not get as large of a tip from younger crowds, but that's crap in my case. I tip extremely well, so some service would be nice. After what seemed like forever, someone finally came over and took our orders. Once everyone finished ordering, everyone but Lindsey began to chat back and forth. I don't know why, but I sensed that Lindsey was a little uptight. She really had no reason to feel that way, and she should have known it.

"So, Lindsey, how's you're brother doing?"

A nice easy question that I thought might break some of the tension she was giving off. Obviously, I was wrong because she gave me this look like, ***What the _____ is wrong with you***? (Feel free to fill in the blank.) Well, I couldn't let things go the way they were beginning to head. So I did the first thing that came in my mind. I picked up a roll and threw it at her. It just seemed like a good idea, and I thought it would lighten her up a little bit. Apparently I was right, because right after it struck her on the nose, she cracked a smile.

"Lindsey, would you like some butter with that?"

She began to laugh, and I felt the tension ease up.

After they brought out our salads, the waitress asked me the big question.

"Would you like shredded cheese on your salad?"

"Hell no, umm sorry, I mean, no thank you."

77

I don't fall for the same trick twice. Hattie, however, did get it. My goal was to get out of there for under fifty dollars. Just then, they asked me if I would like fresh ground pepper on my salad. Hattie, once again, went the opposite route as me and got the pepper. Seriously though, what's wrong with the pepper on the table? As the dinner progressed to the main course, everyone was enjoying themselves. Then May said she needed to go to the bathroom. Ok, no big deal, but as she went, all the females at our table joined her. Ladies what's up with that? We guys have been pondering this question from generation to generation. Why do girls go to the bathroom in a group? You will never see guys do this. A lot of guys can't even go when there are people around them. I don't know why that is, either, but it happens.

When the ladies arrived back from the restroom, the waitress came over and asked if anyone would like desert. I said we would need to pay our checks because we had to leave soon. But Hattie said, "I'll take the Crème Broleigh." It cost six dollars and twenty-five cents. All it was, was pudding that had, had the top flamed with fire to make it stiff on top. So, since they cook the top, they call it "crème broleigh" and charge you so much for it.

"Ok, then I'll be back with your dessert and your checks."

Here we go. The moment of truth. Alright, I know I sound like I am the cheapest person alive, but I really am not. I just hate expensive restaurants like that. The food isn't any better there than it is at a regular restaurant. Plus the portions are a heck of a lot smaller. The waitress came back with the pudding, oh wait, "crème broleigh," and our bills. I slowly brought the bill up to eye level. I opened one eye, then the other. Sixty-four dollars. Sixty-four dollars! (Ahh, behold the power of cheese. Shredded cheese: two dollars. Well, what are you going to do?). Thankfully though, they had added the tip into that total, so that made me feel a little better. Not much better, but a little bit.

On our way out, I decided to grab every free thing that they had out. A couple of mints, some toothpicks, and a pack of matches. I think that makes us even for the bill. Ian and I walked back to pick up the van, which wasn't real easy to find because it was dark now. Once in the van, we went back and picked up the rest of our group. We were now on our way to the actual Homecoming dance. As the ladies once again began chatting about their dresses and hair, we guys began discussing bills. It turns out that I got out of there with the largest bill. Doesn't that figure? What were the odds of that happening?

We pulled into the parking lot of the high school. I noticed an extremely large line of people in front waiting to get in. I parked the van and everyone got out and headed for the line. Except for Hattie, she came over to me and stopped me.

"Thank you for dinner."

"You're welcome," I replied.

She then started kissing me. I leaned back up against the van as we basically started making out right there in the parking lot. This night was just getting better and better. I couldn't wait to see what would happen next. After about ten minutes of enjoying each other's company, we headed into the line that had been cut into about half since we had arrived. We waited in line with my arms wrapped around her stomach as she rested her head on my shoulder. *My gosh, this is what love feels like, I thought to myself.*

Chapter 12

As we handed over our tickets, I could see that our entire group was already inside. They were all in another line. This line was for the Homecoming picture. As Hattie and I entered the building, I began to let my eyes wander around. The theme for Homecoming was "Millennium" and apparently, in the year two thousand, everyone was supposed to be broke. The walls were lined with black garbage bags, and aluminum foil, and it was all outlined with duct tape. You could just tell that the people who did the decorations put no effort into it at all. If I had wanted to see a mess like this one, I would have gone to either my own bedroom or a landfill for the dance.

Hattie pulled me over into the picture line. May and Jeff were getting their pictures taken as we entered the line. Jeff was smiling a lot. For some reason, May was not. In fact, she looked kind of upset. I put my arms around Hattie and told her that May looked upset. We both agreed that we would talk to May and find out what was going on after we got our picture taken. When we finally reached the front of the line, the photographer centered us in front of the background. The background was a picture of some fairy tale land with a castle. The sky was a mix of purple and blue, and it did not match what we were wearing at all. The flash went off. I blinked.

"Excuse me, sir, I blinked."

The photographer looked at me for a moment then replied. "It doesn't matter. Next!"

Hmmm ok, why would it not matter? Whatever. When we left the line, May grabbed Hattie and took her to the restroom. I went and stood next to Jeff.

"What's up, Jeff?"

"I just asked May to be my girlfriend."

"Wow, really good for you, Jeff. What did she say?"

"She just told me she needed to think about it."

Ok guys, I hate to break this to you, but when girls want to think about it, it's a no. If they liked you as much as you like them, they would say "yes" right away.

May and Hattie exited the restroom together, and now instead of upset, May looked ticked off. I mean really ticked off.

"Everything all right ladies?" I asked.

Hattie replied, "Everything is fine."

May looked at me like she was going to cry. Gosh, this girl's emotions change quickly, I thought to myself.

"Well, why don't we go join the others and dance?"

I figured I would have a few minutes later with May, and we would be alone and we could talk.

Heading into the gym, they had the rap music blasting. In fact it was so loud that the only way you could hear someone was if you talked directly into their ear. Ian, Chrissie, Lindsey, and Bill had a little circle going where they were all trying to dance. All of us joined in and tried to dance as well. Hattie and I did what I like to call the premarital sex dance. You all probably call it grinding. I call it the premarital sex dance because that's pretty much what you are doing except you got clothes on. After twenty minutes of grinding and dancing, we all took a break and headed back out into the lobby.

I noticed Jeff and May were not talking. May still looked like she was going to cry. As we all headed back into the gym, we all went separate directions. They were playing slow songs finally, so Hattie and I finally got to dance normally and just hold one another in each other's arms and kiss a little. I was in complete paradise. If I were to have died at that moment, I would have died happy. Entering our third slow song in a row, I saw May exit the gym, by herself.

"Hattie, I'll be right back, ok? I have to do something."

"Ok. But who should I dance with?"

"There's Ian and Chrissie. Just hang with them for a couple of minute's, ok?"

"All right, come back soon."

With that, I headed out to find May. She was nowhere in the lobby to be found. All but one hallway was blocked off, so I headed down the open one. As I turned the corner, I saw a girl sitting down with her knees up, her arms around her knees, and her head down in between them both. It was May, and she was crying.

"May, what's wrong?" She just cried, so I asked again.

"May, what's wrong?"

She looked up at me with tears running down her face. I sat down next to her and put my arms around her.

"This is about Jeff asking you out isn't it?"

"Michael J, I told him that I did not like him that way, and now he is all upset at me. I just ruined his Homecoming."

"Aww May, at least you were honest with him so he won't expect anything from you."

"You are right, Michael J, but I still feel really bad about it."

"Hey, May, he may be mad now, but he will get over it. Just don't let it ruin your Homecoming."

"You're right."

"Of course I am right, May. When have I ever been wrong? Now see that wasn't so bad. Now quit crying, and lets' get out there and have some fun."

"That is not the only thing I am crying over."

"Huh? What else is wrong, May?"

"I can't tell you what else."

"Why not. It cant be that bad."

"I am sorry, Michael J, I can't. But I need you to remember something."

"Ok, May, anything you need. I am there for you. That's what friends are for."

"Please, don't say that. Just remember that, no matter what happens tonight, your friendship means so much to me, and I care for you a great deal and would never do anything to hurt you."

"I know that already, May."

"Just remember it. Promise me you will."

"Ok, I promise I will, May."

We both got up and walked back into the gym. The time was flying by. We only had about thirty minutes left until it would be over. I told Hattie what had happened with May.

"Did she say anything else?"

"No, not really. Why Hattie?"

"Just wondering. I am worried about her, too."

Hattie and I danced up a storm together. Both of us were having a great time. Even May and Jeff were dancing together, trying to enjoy it. As they played the last three songs they were all slow songs.

After the first one, I danced the second one with May. Jeff danced with Hattie.

"May, is everything cool?"

"Jeff is still upset, but he agreed to not ruin this night. Is everything cool with you?"

"Yes, I am having the time of my life."

"You remember what I told you, right?"

"Yes, of course."

"Don't ever forget, Michael J."

For the last song, we went back to our dates. Hattie and I kissed for most of the song.

"Michael J," she said when the song was over, "I have something I want to tell you."

This was it. The three words I had been wanting to here. After all this time, Hattie was finally going to tell me those three words: I love you. The words I had been waiting to here for so long. Finally my time had come. I felt a tingle in my spine, and my body was filled with excitement. I was ready, more

88

than ready. I calmed myself down and said, "Ok let's go outside, I can't hardly hear in here, it is so loud."

We exited the gym, and the lobby, because it was loud and filled with people, too. I could not wipe the smile off my face as we went out the doors to the outside.

"Ok, Hattie, what did you want to tell me?"

Chapter 13

Twenty years, one month, and four days. It is not a very long time when you consider how long a lifetime is. Let me tell you, though, it is a very long time to wait to be told by someone that they love you. Sure, you hear it all the time from family members and really close friends, but it has an entirely different meaning when it comes from the opposite sex. Especially if you are involved with that person too. Is there a better feeling in the world? I don't think there is, and after all this time, it was finally my turn. My turn to be the one on the receiving end.

"So, what did you want to tell me?"

As I stood there with her hands in mine, I began to think of all we had been through. From the band trip, our break-up, our getting back together, my falling in love with her these past months. She looked so beautiful standing there with the biggest smile on that I had ever seen her with. Then she opened her mouth. This would be it, the three words I had been waiting for: I love you.

"Michael J, I wanted to wait until the dance was over to tell you this, because I thought it would be more special that way."

"Yes, go ahead," I replied with utter joy. Hattie was still smiling.

"Michael J, I don't like you. I used you for a date to the dance. Made you fall in love with me and Now we are even."

"What?"

"You heard me."

With that, all my hope and dreams had just came to and end. The one thing I had wanted to hear had been used against me.

"You're kidding me, right?" I said with a panicked voice.

"We're even," Hattie replied again.

Hattie went back inside to the lobby. Our group had been sitting waiting area but they were no longer there. A tear began to fall from my right eye as I turned around and walked to the end of the sidewalk and sat on the curb. My head hanging down, I began to cry from the unbearable pain. It hurt more than any bruise or cut I had ever received. This one bruised my heart. What the heck just happened to me. I had just been used. She knew that I would fall in love with her, and she used it to hurt me. I wanted to leave, to just get in the van and drive. I wouldn't stop, either. I just wanted to get as far away as I could. But I thought to myself, *I could not do it, I still have to drive everyone back to my house*. Oh gosh, what was I going to do? All of them were supposed to come chill at my place. I certainly did not want to do it now, but I couldn't just change everyone's plans. Their parents knew they were staying over. Man, how could she do this to me? I had never been told anything like that before in my entire life. How long must she have had this planned out?

Just then I felt an arm put around my shoulders.

"I am sorry, Michael J."

I looked at her with a stare and tears running down my face.

"You were in on this, weren't you, May?"

"No, I swear, I wasn't. I just found out earlier in the restroom."

"Why didn't you tell me May?"

"I couldn't tell you, Michael J. You got to understand, I was in shock over hearing the whole thing and I did not know how to tell you."

"Well I don't know if I believe you, May. Just, please, go tell everyone to come out to the van and we will get out of here."

"I am telling you the truth, but I'll go tell everyone. This conversation isn't over, Michael J."

Ok man, pull yourself together. You can do this. I have to play it cool. I wiped the tears from my eyes, straightened up my tie, and buttoned my sports jacket back up. I took a minute just standing there breathing, getting back my composure. Another tear bean to fall. I was just hurting too much inside. The pain was so great. I wiped the tear off and headed to the van.

Those words, "Now we're even," kept running through my head, over and over again. What kind of person would do something like that and be so hurtful? What hurt even more was the thought that maybe I had deserved it. Maybe this was how she had felt. What I did to Hattie though was not thought out and planned like this was. This was deliberately done with vengeance in mind. What I had done to her was a mistake, yes, but nothing that could even compare to the had my heart was just been ripped out. Now I couldn't even run away from the pain, because they were all coming towards me, as I stood there with the side door open for people to get in. Obviously, at this point, they all had to know, because Hattie probably went in and told them.

We all stood there for a moment. Hattie would not look at me. So I said,

"What's going on? Are we ready?"

"When we get back to your house, Ian and Chrissie are going to drive us home," Lindsey replied.

"Ok, that's cool. You sure?"

"Yeah, we are both tired."

"I can't go home, my parents will wonder what's up," Hattie looked right at me as she said it. *Am I supposed to care*, I thought to myself. Me, being the nice guy I am, and trying to show her that I was not hurt said, "Ok, no problem."

Hattie got in first and went to the back seat followed by Jeff. Then Chrissie gave me a big hug and got in. Ian said, "Tough break. Emperor. you want me to use the force on her?"

"No, it's cool Ian. Get in."

Then Bill followed Ian in. Lindsey stopped and kissed me on the cheek and said, "If you got over me, you can get over this."

I guess that was meant to be helpful and comforting, but it really wasn't. That left May, who apparently would be riding shot gun now.

"I called shotgun inside," May said.

"Whatever," I said, closing the side door.

"We're not done talking. We will finish this at your house. We are not done."

"Ok May."

I opened her door and let her in. I then got in myself, put the keys in the ignition, turned the keys, and headed home. The ride back to my house was very quiet. I think everyone was in shock. I did make sure everyone would still meet for breakfast the next morning.

When we all got back to my house, we all said our good-byes to Ian, Chrissie, Bill, and Lindsey. That left Hattie, Jeff, May, and myself for the entire night. Kind of funny that it was us four left. Jeff and May were not happy with one another either right now. We all went inside into the basement. May said, "Let's go talk." I told her we could go to the living room to talk. Hattie grabbed a blanket, laid down on the couch, and turned on the television. Jeff went upstairs with us after grabbing a blanket. He went into the family room and clicked on the television and laid down. May and I headed over to the living room. She sat in a chair, and I sat on the floor with my back leaning against the wall.

"So, where do we start, May?"

97

Chapter 14

"You still think I was in on it, don't you?"

"Well, May, you haven't proved to me otherwise."

"Michael J, do you remember what I told you to remember? Why do you think I told you that?"

"Maybe you were just trying to cover your butt to not look bad. How long did she have this planned, May?"

"She just told me a little bit about it in the restroom at the dance, but she said she started thinking about it before our dinner double date with Sam. I am so sorry about all this. I feel like it's my fault."

"Why would you think that unless you were in on it, May?"

"I wasn't in on it, I promise you that, but I feel like it's my fault, because I was the one who hooked you two back up."

"That wasn't your fault, May, I wanted one more chance, and I am the one who asked you to do it for me."

"Yeah, but I convinced her, Michael J."

"I think she convinced herself."

"Michael J, do you still think I was in on it."

"I don't know, I don't know anything. My whole life just got thrown upside-down. My heart just got broke by the person I fell in love with. I just don't know what to think about anything right now. How can I ever trust anyone again? How am I to know that they are not just lying to me?"

"You can trust me, Michael J."

"I believe you, May, and I am sorry for doubting you."

I wiped my tears from my face and looked at her face. She had been crying tonight, too. Her eyes were all puffy; you could just tell. We both looked at one another.

"You know, May, if this was the movies, this would be the part where we kiss."

"Yes it would be," she smiled.

"This isn't the movies, though. Thank you for being here for me, May. I really do appreciate it."

"Somebody told me once that that's what friends are for. Besides, Michael J, I did not have anything better to do," she said with a chuckle.

Finally, the frown left my face, and I even gave a little chuckle myself.

"So, what are you going to do about Hattie?"

"There isn't really anything I can do. Obviously, we are through. Other than that, I do not know."

"Michael J, you want me to beat her up?"

"Ha ha, no, that is all right. Besides, she is bigger than you."

"Yes, that is true, but I could still try for you."

"May, it's all good. What are you going to do? You two are supposed to be best friends?"

"She knows that I am really ticked off at her right now. I am going to have to talk to her and work this out obviously. I am also going to make sure she apologizes to you for what she did."

"May, I don't see that happening at all."

"Oh, it will happen, Michael J. I'll make sure of that."

"How are you going to do that, May?"

"When I talk to her, I will make it quite clear that I can't be her friend anymore until she first apologizes to you. So, she will do it. She might not mean it, but she will do it."

"She won't mean it, May. I think that is a given."

"You are probably right. Other than that, the only thing I can do is be mad at her for a while. I guess we could spit in her food the next time she comes to Burger King. I am just kidding."

We both smiled and laughed again. I was really beginning to feel a little better. It still hurt more than I can explain, but at least May was helping me feel a little better.

"So, May, what's the deal with you and Jeff?"

"Good question, he asked me out while we were in line to get into the dance. I never liked him as more than just a friend. I think me going to Homecoming with him made him think that I liked him more than just friends. So, when he asked, I told him I did not like him that way. He got upset and didn't want to talk to me. You know the rest. He is still pretty upset about the whole thing. At least he agreed to be cool for the rest of the dance, but he does not really want to talk to me now and I feel really bad about it."

"I'll talk to him for you, May. It's always hard for a guy, though, when the girl he likes doesn't like him that way. He will get over it, though."

"What are you going to say to him?"

"Well, May, to be honest I really don't know what I am going to say to him. Other than the usual, 'Hey, at least she wants to be your friend.'

"I just don't want him to be upset at me anymore, Michael J. If you can take care of that, that would be great. I am going to sleep now. I am exhausted."

"All right, I'll go talk to Jeff then do the same."

"Michael J, where do I sleep?"

"You can sleep right here on this couch and I'll hit the floor in here."

"Ok that's good, I'll talk to Hattie now, I guess, before I sleep."

We both gave one another a hug that lasted what seemed like forever and then headed to our next conversations. I was wondering what May was going to say to Hattie. I knew that she was ticked off at her, but I did not know how their conversation would go.

As I walked into the family room, Jeff was still watching TV and lying down on the couch.

"Hey, Jeff, let's talk for a minute."

"Ok, MJ, what's up?"

"Well, May told me what happened tonight, and she said you are not really talking with her now because of it."

"Well, MJ, let me tell you, why would she have gone to Homecoming with me if she did not like me?"

"Because you're her friend, Jeff. You know she did not mean to hurt you. She just thought that you two would have a good time together, and she did not want to say 'no' to a friend when you asked her."

"MJ, I don't see you talking with Hattie?"

"My situation is a little different than yours but I will talk to her in the morning. I just need to let things blow over for tonight. Look, Jeff, bottom line is, she is still your friend and she still cares very deeply for you."

As I was telling him this, I could hear that it was getting a little loud in the basement. I went over to the top of the steps.

"Ladies, can you keep it down a little bit? My parents are trying to sleep."

"Sorry," I heard from both of them.

I walked back over to Jeff, who just looked at me as I sat down.

"Well?" I said awaiting a response.

"You're right, MJ, I'll talk to her in the morning and work it all out. I guess friends is better than nothing."

"All right, Jeff, sounds good. I'll see you in the morning."

"Good night, MJ."

I went back into the living room and laid down on the floor. I was tired, but I really wanted to hear what was going on with May and Hattie. I thought about how May was probably letting Hattie have it good. It kind of comforted me for a few minutes. Talking with Jeff took my mind off my own issues, even if it was just for a short period of time.

After about another half an hour, May came back upstairs to the living room and laid on the couch.

"Well, May, what happened?"

"You need to talk to her about it, ok, Michael J?"

"All right, I can accept that. And I smoothed things over with Jeff for you. He will talk to you in the morning."

"Michael J, can we just talk for a while, not about relationships."

"Sure."

For two hours, May and I stayed up talking about anything and everything except relationships. We both needed it, to feel normal for a while and to take the stress off our minds. Come morning, we both had another conversation to have, and I was not looking forward to it very much at all.

Chapter 15

As I awoke the next day I glanced at the clock. It was a little after one in the afternoon. I went and cleaned myself up and called Ian. Ian said they just got up too, and we would meet at two-thirty for breakfast. I went around and woke May and Jeff up. I also yelled down the steps and told Hattie to get up. Everyone scattered around the house and did their thing to get ready. I was in my bedroom when I shouted out.

"Hey we are leaving in five minutes, so hurry up."

Making my way back downstairs everyone was ready to my shock. We all looked pretty tired but at least we would be on time. We all walked outside and May got in her car with Jeff. Hattie said she would ride with May.

"No, ride with me, we need to talk and May and Jeff need to talk too."

Fortunately or unfortunately depending on how you look at it she agreed and we both got into the Blue Bomber and took off for the restaurant. Now the restaurant was about two minutes away from my house so there would not be time to get into anything major. Not that it mattered, because neither one of us said a word all the way there. Boy this was going well. I hope May was having a better time than I was.

When we arrived at the restaurant Ian and Chrissie were already waiting outside with Lindsey. I noticed that Bill; Lindsey's date had not come. Apparently he had to work or something like that. May and Jeff must have talked during the two minute trip to the restaurant because you could tell that things were more comfortable. We all got a table and sat down. Somehow Hattie actually sat next to me. Ian and I struck up a conversation about the rumor of Mario Lemieux coming out of retirement (the greatest hockey player ever). All the girls started up there own conversation about something, I am sure was

110

not nearly as important as Mario coming back to play hockey. Despite everything that had happened the night before everyone seemed to be in a good mood and high spirits. The food arrived, everyone was still talking. The same occurred when the checks arrived.

About twenty minutes after the check had come Lindsey decided to leave. Ian and Chrissie did the same. That left May, Jeff, Hattie and I again to ourselves.

"May I noticed you and Jeff seem to be more comfortable today." I replied.

"Yeah, we talked in the car and came to an understanding, what about you two?"

Hattie and I looked at one another.

"Not yet, will talk when I take her home I guess."

"Well Jeff and I have to go I have to be at Burger King at five."

We all exchanged our goodbyes. May whispered into my ear. "Call me later let me know how it goes."

"Definitely, you can count on it," I replied.
We hugged and with that they both left.

"Well umm Hattie, lets go pay the cashier and get out of here."

You know I don't want to say she was scared or afraid because she wasn't. She was just waiting for me to tell her off or something, and the anticipation I think was overwhelming her. I paid the bill and we headed for the Blue Bomber. I opened her door for her and let her in. I have a little rating system of mine of what type of person someone is (thanks to a movie the guys will know). When I unlock their door and let them in if they don't reach over and unlock my door then they are inconsiderate and it shows that she is a stubborn person. I had not noticed it before but she did not unlock my door while I was walking across the car to get in my door. It's usually something I always watch for but I guess since I liked her so much, I had never really noticed it before. As I turned the key and put the Blue Bomber into drive it was time to get it on.

"Well Hattie where do we begin?"
****

This was it, we were about to have it out. I was going to let her have it for the way she broke my heart. I would tell her off like no one has ever been told off before. I would make it even for the night before. To be ready to be told that someone loves you was such a great feeling, and that is what makes it hurt all the more when your heart is ripped out. Hattie was so beautiful, kindhearted, and fun to be with how could she have done this?

"Well Hattie where do we begin?"

She looked at me and was completely silent. Probably wondering what I was going to say to her.

"You know, it was really rude and hurt me very much what you did to me last night. In fact it really ticked me off."

"Ok Michael J I admit that I could have done it a better way."

"A better way, a better way. You planned this out from the beginning of us getting together. So tell me

113

how the _____ (fill in the blank) there could have been a better way."

"All right, I did have it planned but you deserved it."

"For what Hattie, cheating on you?"

"Yes."

"Come on, we went out one time that does not make us boyfriend and girlfriend, plus that is totally irrelevant compared to what your did to me."

"Well, I thought you had it coming," she replied.

"What is that supposed to mean Hattie?"

"Its like I told you last night, now we are even."

"Oh my gosh Hattie, do you realize how much in love with you I was, and still am? Even with what you did to me I still am in love with you. I must be the dumbest person alive. Can you just answer some stuff for me truthfully please?"

"Ok, I guess I owe you that much."

"Do you care for me at all?"

"It was fun, but I don't like you that way anymore."

"So then Hattie, that's it, I guess we are done?"

"Michael J I liked you the first time, you liked me the second time. Maybe we could just try the middle and just try being friends."

"Friends huh."

"Yeah Michael J, friends."

She put her hand out to shake mine. I looked at her for a moment. I began to run our history through my mind and think of what I should do. I went from liking her to loving her now to having consider this handshake and starting a friendship. What's the worse that could happen she would screw me over with friendship?

"All right Hattie."

We shook hands and with that she exited the Blue Bomber and made her way inside. I started on my way home; I grabbed my cell phone and dialed up May who was already at home.

"Well Michael J what happened?"

"How did you know that it was me May?"

"I knew you would call right away."

"We agreed to be friends, somehow I agreed to give it a try."

"I guess that it's a step to being civil to one another Michael J."

"Yes it is a step, but I think it will be cool between us and that we can make friendship work. I just get that feeling for some reason. You know how I am."

"Well Michael J it takes a big person to even agree to something like that after what happened. At least you did get one really good friend out of all this, me."

"Well we are trying friendship."

"Not Hattie Michael J, me."

"You're right May and I am truly grateful for that. Ill see you at work later May."

"All right that care Michael J."

"You too."

So what did I learn from all this? Well to tell you the truth not much. I would fall for the same think all over again. That's what love does to you, it clouds your judgment, manipulates your mind, and decision making. Having true love is the greatest feeling that there is in life, that is why so many people want it. If it was easy to obtain then people would not want it as bad as they do. This is why I will never give up looking for it. Boy, I can't wait for another chance, for true love to begin.

Catch Michael J in his next adventure

"In the beginning there was love."

A prequel to

"Alls fair in love and war."

About the Author

Michael Jason Adams grew up with a loving family and great friends. Writing always seemed to come natural to him. He has had two poems published and plans to publish an entire book of poems one day.

Michael spends most of his time working with children in sports and at risk youths. Any spare time that he has goes to playing hockey, writing, chess, and trying to find that one true love. Michael plans for the future include sequels and a prequel to "All's fair in love and war".

9 781418 411169